TURTLE

MATT PHELAN

WALK

GREENWILLOW BOOKS, *An Imprint of* HarperCollins*Publishers*

Turtle walk. Nice and slow.

Here we go.

Are we there yet?

No.

Turtle walk. Nice and slow.

Here we go.

Are we there yet?

No.

Turtle walk. Nice and slow.

Here we go.

Are we there yet?

No.

Turtle walk.

Nice and s l o o o o w.

Here . . . we . . . go.

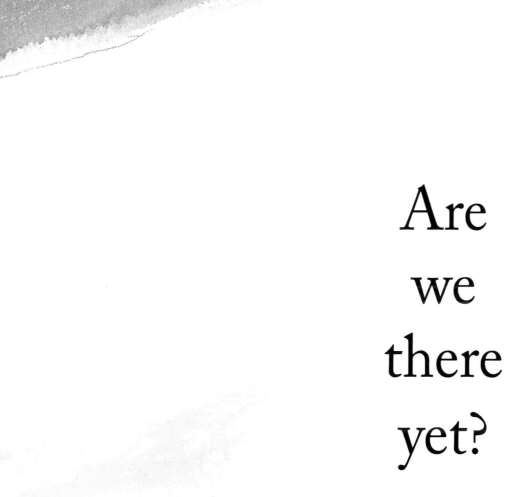

Are
we
there
yet?

YES.

Turtle walk?

Nice and slow?

NO.

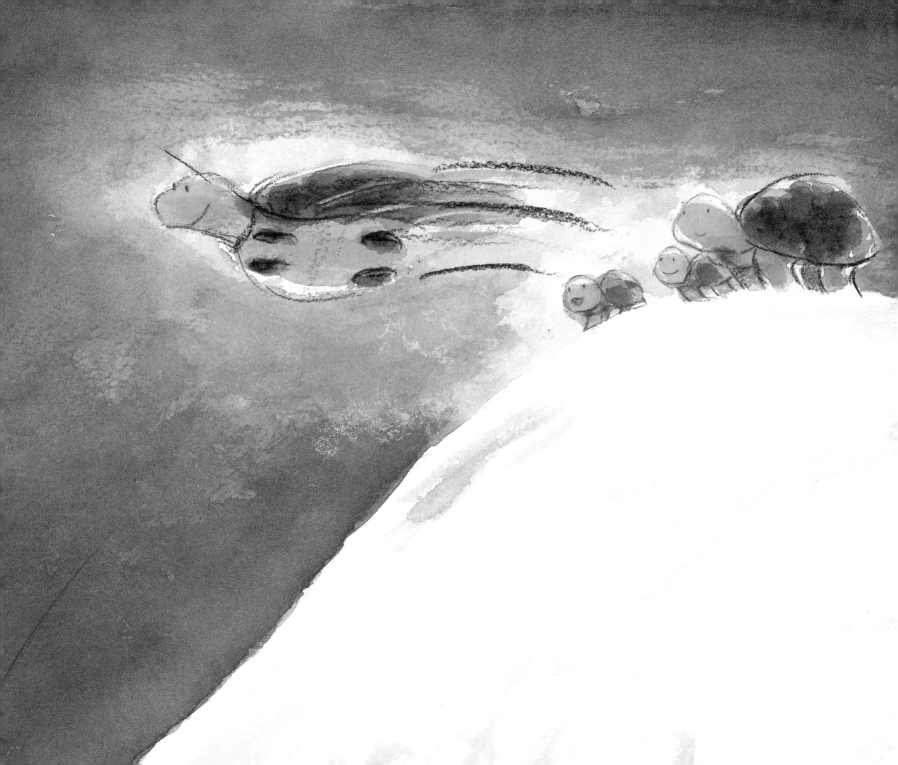

HERE WE GO!

Turtle rest.

Nice and long.

Here we . . .

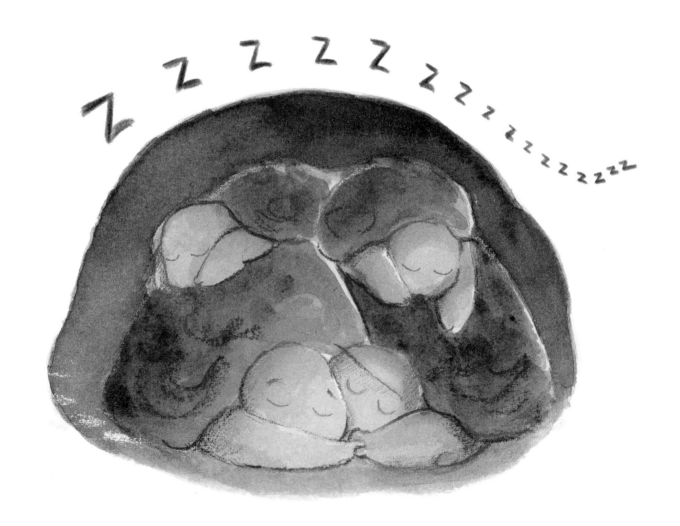

FOR MY FAMILY

Turtle Walk
Copyright © 2020 by Matt Phelan

All rights reserved. Printed in the United States of America. For information address HarperCollins Children's Books,
a division of HarperCollins Publishers, 195 Broadway, New York, NY 10007.
www.harpercollinschildrens.com

Watercolor and pencils were used to prepare the full-color art. The text type is Adobe Caslon Pro.

Library of Congress Cataloging-in-Publication Data

Names: Phelan, Matt, author, illustrator.
Title: Turtle walk / written and illustrated by Matt Phelan.
Description: First edition. | New York : Greenwillow Books, an Imprint of HarperCollins Publishers, [2020] | Audience: Ages 4–8 |
Audience: Grades K–1 | Summary: "A family of turtles goes for a long, long walk that has an unexpected and very fun ending"— Provided by publisher.
Identifiers: LCCN 2019041845 | ISBN 9780062934130 (hardcover)
Subjects: CYAC: Turtles—Fiction. | Walking—Fiction.
Classification: LCC PZ7.P44882 Tu 2020 | DDC [E]—dc23 LC record available at https://lccn.loc.gov/2019041845

21 22 23 24 PC 10 9 8 7 6 5 4 3 2

First Edition
Greenwillow Books